OH MERCENARY ME!

My Unbelievable Life after a Traumatic Brain Injury

Written By James Walker Innes

BIND, I hope you enjoy this
first book of mine!!!...
Especially after you
realize which parts
are true!!!

-jimmy I.

(James Walker Innes)

Dedication

This book is dedicated to my dad who wanted me to tell my story, and to my mother who always told me to, "Reach for the stars!"

Prologue

My service in the military, traumatic brain injury, subsequent injuries listed in this book, childhood, college days, and course of study are actual events. The rest of this book is a biographical crime fiction. I hope you enjoy reading it as much as I enjoyed writing it.

Introduction

To step forth from a strong foundation, I enlisted in the Marine Corps to straighten myself out and get myself that sure footing right out of high school. Having a fantastical view of what my life would be like, I wanted to eventually become a writer. After serving my time in the Marine Corps and then going into the French Foreign Legion, I couldn't put out of my mind that there was probably a life out there that I could create for myself with forty percent imagination and sixty percent hard work. You can continue reading to find out what choices are available when you're touched by that fickle finger of fate.

PhotoScan by Google Photos

1

August 30, 1988—Graduation Day from Parris Island

Platoon ten-sixty-seven dismissed! I stepped back with my left foot in unison with the Marine to my left and the Marine to my right. All 200 plus new Marines of our series 1064 with Platoon 1067 yelled, "Aye aye sir!"

I had just become Private Innes United States Marine Corps Reserve. I went through recruit training at MCRD (Marine Corps Recruit Depot) Parris Island, South Carolina three months ago weighing 185 pounds with considerably more hair than I have now! Now, I weigh 167 pounds and have a scar from four stitches running vertically up my forehead from the corner of my right eyebrow where it touches the top of my nose.

This scar was from one of the many injuries that can be incurred while learning to use crew served heavy weapons. We were snapping in (assuming the firing position), and upon being given the command to move, the pair of us would run in and dive behind the M60. When I dove in, my head hit the butt of the M60, but I continued snapping in. A drill instructor from another platoon yelled, "Stop! That motivates the hell out of me!"

When all of the other drill instructors were looking at me in the firing position behind the M60 with blood streaming down my face from my forehead, the same drill instructor said, "This recruit hit his head, saw that he was bleeding, and continued snapping in!"

Teaching boys to be Marines has its perils to say the least! I was a newly graduated United States Marine. I didn't think or wonder how long I was going to have to apply my new definition of discipline in my life. I just did it. On Parris Island, "Discipline is the instant willing obedience to orders and respect for authority." Being in the reserves, I had a month before I had to check into my duty station prior to attending my Military Occupational Specialty School (MOS or job) next summer.

PhotoScan by Google Photos

Being in the Marines motivated me to be a 0311, which is a basic rifleman. Furthermore, this had me continue along with the basic Marines job description of,

"To locate, close with, and destroy the enemy by fire, and maneuver and to repel the enemies' assault by fire and close combat."

I did not have any time to take the ten days every new Marine has to unwind (a person in the military gets 2.5 days of leave for every thirty days served). I was already accepted into Thrice Won (a very prestigious Military Academy in New Hampshire). I was leaving Marine Corps Recruit Training to join the recruit training and take courses at Thrice Won. This academy was named after the three major wars that the United States had won: the American Revolution, the War of 1812, and the Civil War. It was established after the Civil War to heal the fractures created from the commanding officers. They all knew each other and learned their profession together. However, this did not stop them from going at each other's throats.

Within hours of my graduation from Parris Island, I flew from Savannah International Airport to Boston Logan Airport. My father had driven my car and left it there for me a few days before my arrival. I drove several hours to the academy that is near Littleton New Hampshire. It is located high in the hills and very secluded.

I completed three months of learning to push myself beyond exhaustion in the Marine Corps recruit training. This helped me get to Thrice Won by 10pm. The few who were awake were still in uniform. They were mainly the sentries and the Officer of the Day at the main administration building. My company sergeant was called, and he told me to follow him. I saw his rank being three Chevron's up with two hanging bars. I knew from my recent Marine Corps recruit training that he was an E-7.

I quickly said, "Yes sir Gunnery Sargeant!"

He sternly told me, "I am not a sir, and I don't know what a Gunnery Sargeant is. I'm a Sargeant First Class! Grab your gear and follow me."

We then walked down the parade ground to my barracks which I found out later was Delta Company. This was to be my new home for the next year and a half.

Thrice Won provided me a chance to unwind after Parris Island. There was an introductory German class that met five days a week. My family, *mutterlicherseits* (which is German and means on my mother's side) all originated on a farm in Switzerland. I wanted to be able to speak with my family ever since I lost my Uncle Hans when I was eleven years old, but couldn't because I didn't speak German.

I was in the United States Marine Corps Reserve while also being a college student. The discipline of being a Marine meant I did not have a problem attending all of my classes, and I had the resolve of completing all of my daily homework. I would practice my German as often as I could. I also wrote my mother letters in German, and she would correct them before mailing them back to me.

One other advantage to being in the reserves while attending college is that once a month, I went to drill where I continued with my Marine Corps task of " To locate, close with and destroy the enemy by fire, and maneuver and to repel the enemies assault by fire and close combat." I also received one hundred dollars that wound up being beer money for the weekend. I competed for and won a scholarship to college through the United States Marine Corps. This happened at the same time that I decided that German language and literature would be my major.

Thrice Won is a science and engineering school, but I wanted to study a foreign

language. I was awarded the Cadillac of scholarships by the Navy with the Marine

Corps option, so I transferred to Boston University to pursue my linguistic studies in

my sophomore year of January 1990.

§

I had a blast being a young Marine in college in Boston--the cradle of our

American Revolution. I had the best linguistic training for German there, and I had

over thirty six colleges and universities to go to for a different party and different

women every weekend. I also took advantage of the many job opportunities

available. I worked for one season at the Old Boston Garden (the year before it was

torn down) and got to see every Celtics and Bruins game for free while walking up

and down the balcony yelling, "Hey! Popcorn, candy bars, and peanuts right here!

You want 'em, we got 'em!"

That job was preceded by four months of working at Bonsai West in Littleton,

Massachusetts. As cool as it sounds to work in a bonsai nursery, I did no pruning or

selling, but instead, combined two separate eight-foot-high dirt piles into one pile

with a shovel, and I also moved heavy as hell bonsai plants wherever they wanted

them. On August 30, 1988, I had no idea my Marine Corps training would be utilized

this way!

Since I had such an outstanding memory, I was always exempted from my

exams. While everyone else was studying, I used that time to run about four to six

miles in the morning and then proceed to drink beer the rest of the time. Being a motivated student and being drunk most of the time prompted me to go to some of my exams anyway! I was thrown out of three exams for being too drunk to write my name and still had an A for that semester.

2

Most people have one or two ways of remembering their childhood. It was either healthy and happy or troubled and unhappy. My childhood fell under the healthy and happy category. My parents were hands on and created a stable environment for me and my younger brother and older sister. I have a great relationship with my brother and don't have a close relationship with my sister. My brother is much smarter than I am, and I always admired and respected him for that. Family dynamics are interesting. I am the middle child, and we can philosophize about that all day long.

I was born in Doylestown, Pennsylvania in 1969. We spent four years in Connecticut after moving there when I was three and that preceded our move to Georgia. I spent most of my life in Georgia with copious amounts of time spent in Switzerland where my mother's family provided her a much-needed break from having to watch us. I did a brief stint in boarding school in New Hampshire where I was thrown out of for drinking when I was eighteen. This provided me my first lesson in Marine Corps history and my first motivational Marine Corps speech. My recruiter called me and said the Marine Corps doesn't care if you drink as long as you finish high school because the Marine Corps was founded in a bar called Tun Tavern in Philadelphia in 1775.

The recruiter provided me with a speech that stayed with me throughout everything you're going to read about in this book. He told me, "Every now and then, life's going to hit you between the eyes and knock you flat on your back. In the Marine Corps, you will learn to get up and keep marching."

My father was born in the United States and my mother immigrated here from Switzerland. She spoke fluent German, and her mother's side of the family are farmers.

When I was six or seven, I would filch drinks from family events where alcohol was always served, and my younger brother would follow my lead. I started drinking alcohol a lot more in the sixth grade, and my grades had fallen as the partying increased. I realized that I could get away with more if I was as good of a student as I was before. In my sophomore year of high school, I really buckled down on studying. History, geography and English were my strong subjects, and I was on the High Honor Roll through the rest of high school.

I was a shy extrovert, but it didn't stop me from having many friends. I excelled at solo sports such as swimming, running, and tennis. I played rugby later on in college, and when the ball was given to me, I just ran with it. All of the running and rugby made the Drink Ups easier to survive. The Drink Ups were celebratory times of imbibing where the teams would get together following a match. One other thing, the Drink Ups kept rugby a club since no college can sanction that kind of drinking.

I graduated in 1988 and looked forward to life outside of school. That's why I enlisted in the Marine Corps. I wanted to get a solid foundation from which to step off.

Every kid has their dream of doing something one day. I wanted to be a writer. Maybe I would write something that could have a positive effect on someone else. I did know that you couldn't be a writer if you didn't have any experiences to write about. Hence, the Marines.

PhotoScan by Google Photos

3

One of my best friends at Boston University was Grigori Pushkin. He was another hopeful future Marine Corps officer on scholarship with the Marine Corps. His family emigrated to the United States from Moscow in the early '70's. Grigori and I were college roommates for two years at Boston University. I studied a foreign language, and he studied mathematics. I was the outgoing forward one, and he was the steadfast serious one. In my senior year, I walked into our kitchen (we rented a house off campus) with some questions for Grigori. He was sitting at our kitchen table eating some Granny Smith apples and Entenmann's cookies (his favorites!). Those are what his parents had for him when he went home to do laundry every weekend.

"I know your family emigrated to the United States in the 70's. What year was that?"

"1976."

"What does your father do? "

"He's a chemical engineer."

"How many of your family members immigrated with you?"

"All four of us. I was only six at the time. I have no more relatives there."

I then told him that Leonid Brezhnev was the Secretary General of the Soviet Union in 1976 (he's the same person who is part of a government that had Nikita Khrushchev beating his shoe on the desk of the United Nations in 1960), and he was not part of a tolerant government.

"Your entire family was part of that regime and they were able to leave and live in their country's biggest enemy?"

"Yes."

"And your father was part of the intelligentsia that had been trained by the government?"

"Yes."

"How did your family pull that off?"

"Heady Glympton."

"Who's that?"

"He's a high placed government official."

"How so?"

"He's a governor of a state in the United States."

§

A few months later, Grigori and I were throwing one of our parties. These were a big deal for us and the college community. We spent the entire morning thoroughly cleaning our house, or as the Marine Corps refers to it as, "Field Day." Being the college students we were, we got a keg of beer along with three or four quarts each of Pepe Lopez Tequila and Cossack Vodka. I chose these hard liquors because I liked the picture on the bottles!

There were about three hundred people in attendance when a tall middle-aged man in a nice suit came in with an entourage of celebrities. There was one who

17

resembled a comic book character Johann Minx, a mercenary, who I continuously read about over a decade before when I was eleven or twelve. I was bitten by the bug to become a soldier of fortune. There was also—get this!—Johann Goethe, the mobster of the Green Foot. I saw him as the ultimate self-made man.

It was my party and I was quite drunk. I went up to the middle-aged man in the suit and asked him outright if he was a professor at Boston University. He told me, with the greatest confidence, that he was Heady Glympton, a United States governor.

I countered with, "You're a politician?"

"Yes."

I'm fairly sure that there was quite a bit of disdain in my voice, and my fist immediately connected with his right cheek. That punch had tremendous consequences. He told me that I would regret my rash actions unless I went AWOL (ABSENT WITHOUT LEAVE) with him right now. He immediately left my party with his twenty or so people. Grigori told me that I probably made a huge mistake and suggested that I go after Heady to find out what he wanted from me.

This so-called governor promised me that if I didn't leave with him and abandon my college life and the Marine Corps right then, he would ruin my life so that he could rebuild me in his image to become a powerful leader. I was quite right to be skeptical of this man's claim to be a high placed government official, but ashes to ashes, dust to dust, the proof of the pudding is under the crust. He did have Johann Goethe with him, and that was no small deal since this hero of mine served time in a federal prison following his betrayal by a trusted advisor.

When Heady left my party, it prevented me from getting to talk with two of my heroes who helped guide my life thus far. Johann Minx and Johann Goethe. The Marine Corps provided me with a stable foundation and also provided me with worthwhile combat skills so I could become a mercenary like Johann Minx. Now here he was! I had never been able to figure out how I can get my foot in the door of the mercenary world.

Johann Goethe was nicknamed the Elastic Earl by the media. They wrote about his exploits of always being able to bounce back from various attempts by the government to indict him for any crime while also foiling multiple assassination attempts on his life, or bouncing back like an elastic band. I would dedicate as much time as a mercenary as it would take to become a well-known fighting man who had the necessary abilities in order for me to pledge my allegiance to Johann Goethe, head of one family in the German crime syndicate the Green Foot.

This name, the Green Foot, is derived from the battle of Teutoburg Forest in 9 A.D. when an alliance of Germanic tribes ambushed and annihilated three Roman legions (or 15,000 men) at 5,000 Roman soldiers per legion. This is what they do—ambush and destroy people, lives and anything else that didn't derive a profit for them.

4

At midnight on May 9, 1992, I was trying to get on the tram car known as The T. This tram stopped running regularly at midnight of Saturday to midnight of Sunday. I was going about four miles to the punk bar, The Rathskeller, in Kenmore Square to do some slam dancing. I was already drunk and in a big hurry. In my haste, I ran across Commonwealth Avenue in Boston and a car hit me on my right leg. The impact broke my tibia, fibula, right wrist and forearm and knocked my right arm out of its socket. This all preceded my head eliminating half of the windshield of the car. This became my entry ticket into the traumatic brain injury survivor group.

PhotoScan by Google Photos

While in the ambulance on the way to Brigham and Women's Hospital, I was sedate after having my brain scrambled against a windshield. I began to rouse as soon as I got to the hospital. In order for me to not be thrashing around while they saved my life, I was put into a medically induced coma.

They had to perform a tracheotomy (an operation of cutting into the trachea to deliver oxygen safely to the lungs). I'm telling you my friends this is the one scar I don't mind keeping since it shows I went to hell and back in a different sense than what the Marine Corps took me through.

Not to bore you with my long list of injuries, but both of my lungs were shredded in this accident. To prevent my lungs from filling up with fluid, I was put in a bed that followed a U shape. It had the mattress on its left side that then moved to a flat position and then came up onto its right side. Then it was repeated in the opposite direction. The movement was very limited because the tracheotomy tube and the twenty three machines I was hooked up to could not be shaken loose.

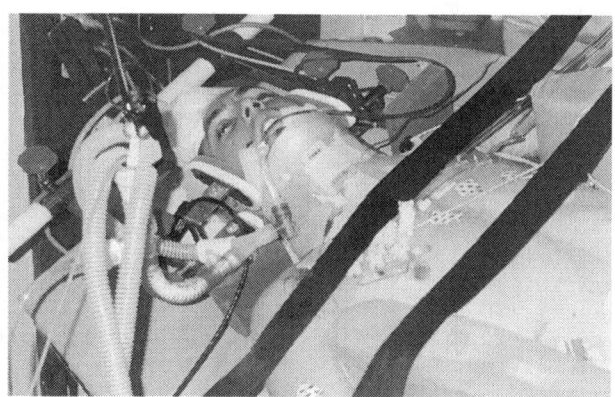

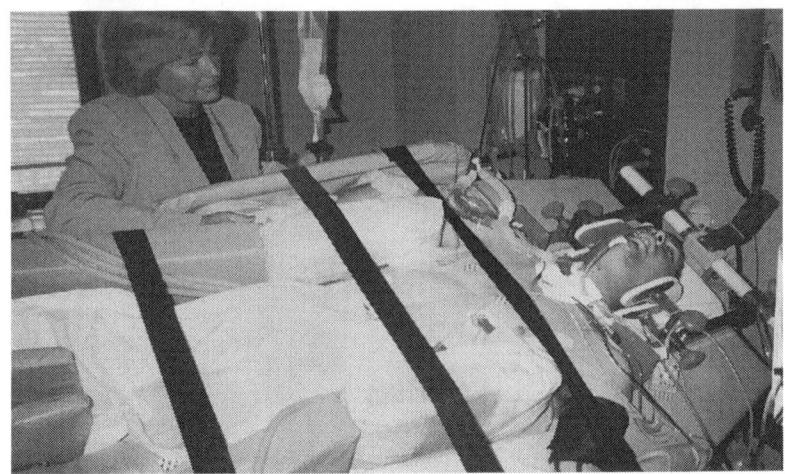

PhotoScan by Google Photos

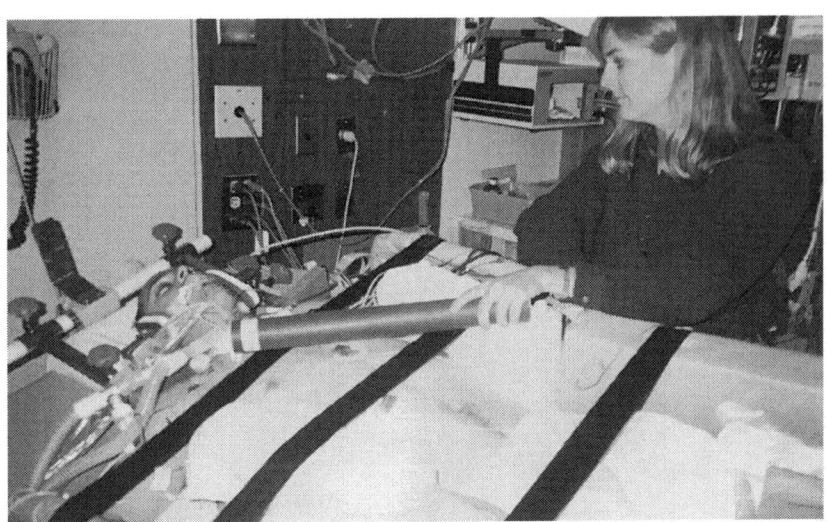

PhotoScan by Google Photos

It took two months for me to come out of the coma. I know that no longer being comatose sounds like a light and uplifting part of my story, but I am not certain where the sad tragic part of my story ends. I was awake but had to constantly work on walking, talking, social interaction, memory, controlling any and all impulses, and maintaining my stamina, concentration and wakefulness in order to continue living as an independent adult. If you never had to relearn these basic skills for a second time in your life, you can't relate to how grueling this is.

After a traumatic brain injury, your mind plays games with you. In my mind, I went on a world tour! When people would come to visit me, I would ask them how they got to Switzerland or Australia or California or any other place I came up with. One of the most difficult things to get used to was being wheeled around in a wheel chair. I went from being able to walk, run and bike to this. My thought processes and emotions were helter-skelter to say the least! I am fairly certain that these circumstances would weigh heavily on anyone but, as I already knew, one U.S. Marine is never outnumbered and, therefore, never defeated.

§

Whatever constitutes the substance of your life, up until the point of your traumatic brain injury, is what you have as your strengths going forward. A brain injury is invisible. Many times, there are no visible scars or missing limbs to give people a head's up that something is amiss. People tend to think that the person with the injury is messing with their head by not remembering things or coming up with weird stories. The truth is that the person before the brain injury is not the same person now. He or she will have to find their new normal. This is very tough for family members and loved ones to grapple with. I was on my way to a nightclub to go slam dancing and possibly land some tail, and now here I am happy to walk twenty yards without becoming winded and confused.

I had absolutely no energy to do anything. I slept sixteen hours a day (this is typical and should be expected following a traumatic brain injury). The other eight hours of the day were consumed by my rehabilitation—speech therapy, physical therapy, occupational therapy, recreational therapy (card, board and memory games). I had lunch for one hour each day, and that was very welcome particularly because it was followed by a nap and then a visit from my mother.

I also took an ambulation class. Ambulation comes from the Latin verb *ambular* (meaning to walk). With my brain rewiring itself from the force of the impact, I forgot my Latin training from eight years ago. I told my family when they came to visit that I was in an amputation class and that they were going to cut off my leg! My family reassured me that if they were going to cut off my leg, they would have done so already.

I did not have many complaints from anyone except my dear mother who desperately wanted me to talk. When I was talking again, I didn't realize that I lost three and a half years worth of recent memory. However, I was still able to speak German after my mother prompted me. I also had one of my Marine Corps drill instructors tell me in a dream, "You got hurt. So what. All you can do now is keep moving."

It took over three months of talking to people to accept that I was hit by a car as a pedestrian, but my mind couldn't wrap itself around this. My conversations with others went something like this:

"What happened to you?"

"I was shot."

Someone else asked, "What happened to you?"

"I was in a hang gliding accident."

"No Jimmy. What really happened to you?"

"I was hit by an airplane."

As you can tell, I didn't know which end was up. I bragged about talking to famous people. I even told them that Heady Glympton, President of the United States, visited me four months before he ran for office.

§

Having a traumatic brain injury left me with some deficits, one of them being forgetfulness. Although, the one thing I didn't forget about was drinking. I told one lady who visited me frequently that I would be able to drink alcohol again once I was off the high blood pressure medication. I considered not drinking a deficit, but not sure how many other people would. Alcohol is a destabilizing drug. I couldn't see that I was already unstable, so why shouldn't I drink?

I also wore my emotions on my sleeve. This created circumstances where the slightest word, comment, or action would enrage rather than mildly annoy, and bring tears of sorrow rather than mild irritation. My traumatic brain injury will be with me the rest of my life. I will always be working with these deficits. They still influence me, twenty eight years later, by how much I do or don't eat, do or don't sleep, do or don't exercise, do or don't do anything.

I was in intensive therapy for two months at Brunswick Hospital in Amityville, New York. Heady came to visit me during his campaign to become President. People still considered this to be my imagination. He still had the same entourage of celebrities with him. I had a vague recollection of all of them, but couldn't figure out in my addled mind why celebrities were in my hospital room.

"Who are you?" I asked Johann Minx.

He answered my question with a question. "Who do I look like?"

I continued our dialogue of question with question with, "Why did you come here?"

"Because the next President of the United States asked me to come."

Heady Glympton became President that year.

After completing my therapy in early September of 1992, I was finally able to go back to the small southern city in Georgia where I spent most of my life. However, therapy was far from over for me. I did two and a half years of outpatient therapy in Georgia at Memorial Hospital for four months, Meadowbrook in Atlanta for five months, and Second Chance in Savannah for four months. My rehabilitation from brain injury was interrupted at times by being gainfully employed at various companies, all of which I was fired from. I either drank my way out of them or I was just an ass bag.

§

I excelled in my therapy and this made me feel that I could be more than just a patient. As a result of my injury, I was fired from six paying jobs and eleven volunteer jobs. The first paying job I had after returning to Savannah in the beginning of 1993 was at a company named Hydrau-Bear (which was a US subsidiary of Mann and Hummel). I was making $500-$600 per week sending auto parts from a warehouse in North Carolina via phone and fax, but the traumatic brain injury will always influence my decision processes. After working there for five months, I got up and told them I'm going to eat lunch. They asked me when I was going to come back, and I told them I'm not. I went on a plane that afternoon to visit my younger brother in Boston. There was no good reason for me to leave a high paying job. This was the first of many jobs where I became a non-entity after I was no longer welcome.

On the volunteer jobs, one veteran's hospital in Atlanta was so large that I kept getting lost every time they sent me somewhere. When they sent me on another assignment, I had to ask for directions to get back to the volunteer headquarters. I did get fired from one volunteer job at the Humane Society. It was a simple job. All I had to do was pet cats and walk dogs. Apparently, they didn't think I could do it drunk!

I was given a chance, years later, to have a physical at NAS (Naval Air Station) in Beaufort, South Carolina. One part of the copious amount of forms I had to fill out had me list all scars, broken bones, injuries and surgeries. I realized then that I was no longer military material when I had to ask for a second page! The traumatic brain injury eliminated me from service because it was considered a one hundred percent disability.

Doing so well in therapy made me think that actual schoolwork wouldn't be very hard. In the fall of 1994, I took some paralegal classes at a local college in Georgia. I went in the fall, winter and spring. As a result of my traumatic brain injury, studying was extremely difficult. To combat this, I recorded every class while writing a copious amount of notes. Each night, I listened to the recordings and updated my notes accordingly.

My father, who spent over twenty years as a Naval Aviator, became a lawyer in 1971. I really admired his verbal expertise. I heard him talking to someone on the phone one day. He told that person, "I didn't call you a liar, I just don't think you're telling me the truth." I would love to have that kind of cat and mouse mental agility. This spurred me on with my plan to eventually become a lawyer too. Since I knew I would never become a lawyer in the normal time frame, I did the next best thing to honor my dad by becoming a paralegal instead.

Since I had taken three terms in a row, I took the summer term off. As things seem to always go for me, I was touched by that fickle finger of fate yet again. I was hit by a car as a pedestrian a second time in August 1995. During the four months of recuperation, my leg healed from thirty-three breaks between my knee and ankle.

I knew how difficult it had been for me the first time so I wasn't looking forward to putting myself back into that grind again after being on my back for four months while being waited on hand and foot. It was then that I decided being a paralegal was out of my reach. I felt bad that I disappointed my father. I knew in my heart that not succeeding in this endeavor would make me stronger to succeed in the next.

5

As I already stated, forgetfulness is a key deficit following a traumatic brain injury. In my many conversations with Heady, he reminded me that he promised to ruin my life in order for me to become a great leader under his tutelage. The first thing he said was, "We're going to have to see how you do under pressure while also testing your combat skills."

I quickly interjected, "One U.S. Marine is never outnumbered."

"What about the Rangers you see walking around your Georgia city?"

"It would take at least eleven Rangers to beat one U.S. Marine."

The next morning, there was a knock on the door. I opened the door and saw several men wearing the camouflage utility uniform. I could tell they were not Marines, but soldiers, by the way they folded their sleeves (the Marines roll their sleeves and the Army pushes them up).

"Can I help you?"

"There's eleven of us. Isn't that what you said? It would take eleven of us to beat you?"

I was standing in the doorway, and I realized that I could either step back into the house and slam the door, or remember that it took five thousand U.S. Marines three days to take Tarawa. For those not up on their history, the taking of Tarawa was a great Marine victory. The Japanese government said it would take a million Americans a million years to take Tarawa (Tarawa was a battle in the Pacific Theater in World War II).

I stepped into the middle of them while closing the door behind me. They circled around and started pushing me back and forth between them.

"Cut it out!"

They continued pushing me. I told them, "Stop!"

They continued pushing me and I punched one of them. That's when the fight really started. We were in a confined area, and there was no lack of ability on his part and no exceptional ability on mine. I hit one of them as hard as I could in a particular manner that knocked him to his knees. He was dropped like a bad habit! I immediately knelt down and started to administer first aid.

"Get your hands off him! Stay away from him!"

The ten Rangers who remained picked him up and immediately left. Later on that day, three of the Rangers returned to tell me about the Ranger I hit.

"How is he?"

"He's dead."

"I didn't mean to kill him."

"How does that help his widow and son?"

I went from being a confused traumatic brain injury survivor to a killer and home wrecker. I couldn't tell anyone about it until I realized there were two people I could tell: Johann Minx and Jacko Jaxson.

"Huzzah!" yelled Jacko.

"What does that mean?"

"That's what you say when someone makes their first kill."

"Jacko. I hope you and Johann understand that while I meant to do what I did, I didn't mean to kill him. I had been hit once in a similar manner, but it didn't kill me."

§

Heady, being the one who brought Johann Goethe and eleven Rangers intermittently into my life, had no problem testing me against any other conceivable lethal unit. They all tried to kill me, and I'm the one telling the story, so guess how that went?

My two main mentors that I could not talk about were Heady Glympton and Johann Goethe. They both taught me different things that I had to incorporate into my being. One of the main things that Johann emphasized with me was to be polite. Heady wanted me to be his protégé.

I asked Heady, "Sir, how much longer am I supposed to do this?"

"I'm not through with you yet."

"What are you going to do when I tell the newspapers about this?"

He smiled and said, "What's Jimmy I, who spent months in a coma with a head injury, going to tell people?"

What could I say to that? I said the only thing I could say, "I'm damn proud to serve you!"

My military background, with the strictest discipline known to mankind, made me the perfect candidate to be what Heady needed me to be for his own selfish purposes. Add in my traumatic brain injury and voila! It didn't get any better than that.

I have learned that all people are stones of varying degrees of size that can direct the course that the river of your life flows. Unlike a stone, a person can insert himself into your life again and again and again.

I said the only thing I could, "I'm damn proud to serve you."

I immediately knelt down and started to administer first aid.

6

During my college years, I did find some solace in exercise. I also continued to work on remembering what I learned from the Marine Corps, in addition to studying different techniques used by bodyguards. In the fall of 1994, I was sitting in the student lounge with twenty to thirty others students. The peaceful conversations were broken by a disagreement between two male students. The taller one was bullying the shorter one. After their confrontation ended, I wasted no time going up to the smaller student.

"Listen! Do you want to get that guy to leave you alone?"

"Yeah! What are you going to do about it?"

His quick answer let me know that I was right about his humiliation.

"This is what you're going to do. I want you to walk up to him, point at his face, and say fuck you! You're not bothering me anymore!"

He followed my script perfectly. I knew that the only way you can keep someone from getting injured is if you're more afraid that your client will get hurt than you will. The taller guy immediately reached for "my guy." I stepped between them, grabbed the aggressor's hand and I twisted until he dropped to his knees. After he said he wouldn't bother my "boss" again, I let him go. I realized that bullying really bothered me and was unaware that my anti-bullying strategy was my next endeavor that I would be very proficient and successful at.

This anti-bullying strategy became popular rather quickly around my school and was a moneymaker for me. People knew that if they had a problem, they could turn to Jimmy I. Everyday, for the next four days, I was hired at $20 per hour to arbitrate differences on three separate occasions. I'm glad that I knew how to fight people with various techniques and weapons because I quickly found out that more people carry weapons than you would imagine. I'm not sure if it was due to my traumatic brain injury or my Marine Corps belief that I can't be killed, but I wasn't disturbed that I was putting my life on the line for $20. I had arrived! I was now a bona fide mercenary!!

§

I didn't know that I was already being scrutinized by all the men that go into the mercenary field. Within two weeks, Johann Minx and Jacko (Johann's mercenary mentor) came to visit me. Jacko, in a bragging manner, stated the famous saying, "You've never lived until you almost died. For those who fight for it, life has a flavor the protected will never know." They told me that all the mercenaries didn't appreciate the fact that I was charging $20 per hour when the going price for them was $10,000 per hour. I told them that I couldn't charge $10,000 per hour because I didn't carry a pistol or any other weapon.

I told Johann and Jacko that I was going to continue my very popular mercenary work, but I would stay confined to my small southern city in Georgia. My two mercenary friends didn't have to worry about me continuing too much longer. My college had about enough of my entrepreneurial enterprises. They told me I would be dismissed from school if I continued. So what did I do? I went somewhere else and did it!!

I was standing with Johann and Jacko within arms distance of each other on my front porch when I made the comment, "For international mercenaries, you two don't look so tough." Immediately, they both had knives in their hands and were ready for business. I quickly disarmed them and made their knives drop to the ground. I grabbed the front of Jacko's shirt and pushed him back off his feet while picking up the knife with the longer blade. I put the cutting edge against the skin of his throat and was confident that I had their undivided attention.

"Johann, Jacko is your best friend, your good buddy, right?"

"Yes."

"Well, I want you to prove it to me, unless you want me to cut his throat."

"How?"

"I want you to kiss him on the mouth. You are going to keep kissing him until I tell you to stop. If at any point I think that you both aren't enjoying the kiss, you will be able to describe what it feels like to be kissing someone at the exact moment that they die!"

These two mercenary fighting men went into an amorous kiss. I had them hold it for a count of sixty seconds before I removed the knife and told them to stop. They immediately stopped kissing and started spitting and wiping their mouths with looks of disgust on their faces. I seized the moment thinking I adequately had their attention. You have to strike while the iron is hot otherwise the blade won't be tempered the way you want it to be.

I quickly explained to them, "There is no good reason why I should be able to stand up to either one of you alone, much less be the one dictating the terms of our peace. The two of you are well-known mercenaries. We did not fight. None of us got maimed or killed. Therefore, I don't consider it a fight. I think that we should vow that we will never fight each other and always back each other up in any argument."

We all agreed to my terms. This provided me with training many times throughout my long association with Johann and Jacko. We would be toasting mercenaries with port wine in a crowded public place and one of us would say,

"Vive la morte!"

"Vive la guerre!"

"Vive la sacre mercenaire!"

The translation for this toast is long live death, long live war, long live the cursed mercenary.

Since we were in a military town, any soldiers that were present expressed extreme displeasure at our exuberant behavior. I am trying to keep this story centered around the shit show of living life in the crime syndicate. I'm not going into any of the scuffles that constituted my training alongside these mercenaries and with people on active duty in the U.S. Military.

7

I spent twenty-two years building a foundation with the Marine Corps and getting

my education prior to getting hit by a car the first time. I went back to that as the

most stable ground in the topsy-turvy world that accompanies a traumatic brain

injury. I utilized my Marine Corps training as the best option I had. Stick with what

you know. I used the six troop leading steps called BAMCIS. It means the following:

1. Begin the planning

2. Arrange reconnaissance

3. Make reconnaissance

4. Complete the planning

5. Issue orders

6. Supervise

Begin the Planning needed a public place where alcohol was served that had a lot of young men in the twenty one to thirty five year age group. It couldn't be outside of the military base since the members of the military would be disciplined if they were caught fighting. They also wouldn't be hiring mercenaries. I needed to decide when I would be hiring myself out to arbitrate differences for money. I decided that I would work on Wednesday, Thursday, Friday and Saturday.

Arrange Reconnaissance was accomplished by deciding to go to my "new hangout" on Wednesday, Thursday, Friday and Saturday for three weeks in a row. I would pick a table with the best view of people walking around the various bars and restaurants.

Make Reconnaissance was the easiest part. It's all about the details. I already knew which days I would work. Those were the times when I would sit outside with two ordered drinks on the table so a waiter or waitress wouldn't hassle me. Then, I counted people. I also studied their attire. How many men wore slacks or jeans? What color were the slacks or jeans? How many wore ties? How many wore collared shirts? What color were the shirts? What style of shirt? This would enable me to dress similar to other people and prevent me from standing out.

Complete the Planning was just the "style" I would work. It entailed the following:

- I would look for a clear case of someone being bullied
- I was never paid to injure anyone
- There was never any implication of violence
- I only worked for someone being bullied

- I would never throw the first punch

It was my employer's argument, so they had to be the one doing the talking. If I told a bully to leave someone alone, then it would only bear weight when I was around. That's why all I would do is help my employer stay safe in his negotiations. Each mercenary is an individual army. As a result of my influence and leadership, I was able to keep seventy five to one hundred mercenaries together. We each helped each other instead of being against each other. This had a phenomenal effect in the mercenary world. A well-known international magazine for mercenaries said that I did more for the world of the mercenary than anyone ever had.

After I spent three months arbitrating differences for money, I got the chance to show Johann my mettle. I have always believed in the power of prayer. I prayed that I would be able to show that I am a worthwhile servant for him.

Around 10:30 in the morning the next day, Johann was outside my house with over a dozen men in suits crowding around in a threatening manner. I stepped between Johann and the closest man to him as all the men in suits pulled out a pistol. I swept my right foot under Johann's feet and simultaneously grabbed the front of his shirt to give him a controlled fall. It was no good for me to hurt him while preventing him from being shot. I told him, "Keep your head below waist level!" Now, the only way I could keep him from resuming his position as target was to make myself the center of these gunmen's attention. I disarmed the man closest to me and shot three of his comrades before shooting him. I didn't like loose ends.

It's never easy to remember what happens while you're being shot at as one might imagine. I had to disarm at least three of them, and I found out later that I shot sixteen men. You don't need to know how many you are up against. You just fight until the threat is gone.

When Johann and I were the last men standing, he didn't say 'thanks' or 'nice shooting' or 'way to go' or any other congratulatory statement.

He turned to me and said, "Why did you do that?"

I was more afraid of him than I was of those armed men! My exact words were, "I value your judgment. I want to serve you so that I can learn from you."

"There is a word for what you just said. Do you know what it is?" (Johann is a man of few words)

"No sir."

"Not sir. Johann." he corrected me.

"No Johann, I don't."

"It's called respect." Then he asked me, "What do you want to do?"

"I want to learn by spending more time around you." Then I asked him, "What do you want me to do?"

For an answer, he swept his arm in a semicircle pointing at the men on the ground in various death throes. I immediately told him, "No!"

"What else can you do?"

I then argued with him for quite a while about never wanting to be a hit man. He somehow convinced me that I was of no use to him otherwise. I think that I am fairly smart, but the last fifteen minutes of that first hour had me begging him to let me do what I just said I would never do! Then we got down to the meat and potatoes of my new calling, such as when I am at my peak and what sort of reasons I needed to get into a gunfight. Johann then gave me my first lesson under his tutelage.

"You need to stop dressing like a slob."

I bit my tongue, but not quick enough. "My clothes are always clean!"

The lesson concluded with him telling me, "If you're not wearing a tie, you're a slob."

I explained to him that I never carry any weapons. He just waved his hand at the three or four dead men who were being removed by the "disposal crew." I have no idea what I'd just gotten myself into. The head of a crime syndicate family has to know everything about what's going on in their criminal family in order to control it and negotiate on its behalf. If the head of the family is talking to the heads of other families, they are not "hanging out," they are splitting up influence and various criminal enterprises. When there is a disagreement, they have armed men meet and gain the upper hand at the negotiating table by killing each other! That's how I was to be used.

§

The next day, I had my first example of life as a crime syndicate negotiation tool. I was walking down the street when a car with dark windows pulled up and six men in suits got out and came walking toward me.

"What's up guys? I'm Jimmy I."

"We know who you are. That's why we're here."

I couldn't tell who spoke. That's how things are in the mob. You're never sure who's in charge. The half dozen men lined up facing me. Then, I either heard something or noticed that these men were looking past me, and I turned around and another half dozen men were lining up behind me. As I introduced myself to the ones behind me, someone from the men in front of me said, "Don't talk to them!" The men split in half, six went to my right and six went to my left. I kept looking from one group to the other before I realized my idiocy. I tried to salvage some dignity by saying to the first group, "Oh, are these the guys I'm supposed to kill?"

If you want a complete feeling of powerlessness, understand that I didn't have anything to do with the planning of the timing, location or number of people involved. With that, I back fisted a man from the second group that was standing closest to me. This brought an immediate reaction that surprised the hell out of me. All the men pulled out pistols and started shooting at each other! I had to disarm one of them in order to participate. This was not as much fun as it sounds!

When I saw Johann later that day, I asked him how long I was going to have random gunfights.

"What do you mean?" he said as his brow clouded.

I gave him the only answer that I could. "I'm damn proud to serve you!"

Johann was easily brought into my life by one man. Being able to bring the head of a Green Foot crime syndicate family around me on a regular basis was child's play for the next screw that tightened the lid on my sarcophagus. I mean, at any point of the day, I had to be ready to stand an arms distance away from those who were shooting at me without any retaliation from me until I disarmed one of them!

8

The next confinement in my life came in the form of food and drink. I love spicy food and was not drinking alcohol due to my traumatic brain injury. I began drinking again about a year after my injury even though I wasn't supposed to because I needed the high blood pressure medication I was on. I just doubled up on it before I started drinking. (Author's note: I am a highly untrained professional alcoholic. Don't try this at home). I started drinking a little bit here, a little bit there, which then avalanched into full-blown alcoholism. My intermittent sessions of getting locked up in psychiatric hospitals made it impossible to drink because there was no alcohol there.

Johann told me that the one rule about alcohol in the mob is that "men in the mob don't trust a man that doesn't drink alcohol." He let me know that at any time I was going to hydrate myself, there should be alcohol involved. If I went swimming or biking or did any other type of exercise, I should drink alcohol to replenish the fluids. You and I both know this is ridiculously stupid! This didn't matter because it was all about Johann.

"If I'm going to be in gunfights, wouldn't it be best if I'm not drinking alcohol?"

"We'll take care of that."

Johann hated any form of spice, including salt, and he was an over sixty-year-old alcoholic who had no choice but to stop drinking because alcohol was a no-no in federal prison.   The confinement came in the form that Johann could only eat and drink what I ate and drank! That meant that one of us had to yield. Obviously, that one of us was me. I had to stop eating spicy food and could only frequent restaurants, bars and taverns that serve alcohol.

Johann always supplied an answer to a problem in the most expedient manner possible. The only two characteristics that all his solutions for me had were they were life endangering and extremely violent. He asked me why I did not drink alcohol, even after he told me that the men in the mob don't trust a man that doesn't drink alcohol. I used my ace in the hole immediately.

"How can I be in one, two, three or more gunfights per day if I am drunk?"

"You're about to find out."

The next morning, while it was still dark, Johann showed up like he always did, unexpected and outside the house where I was living. He handed me a six-pack of 16oz. Budweiser cans.

"Drink this."

"How much time do I have?"

"Drink it!"

Even though I can be a clock watcher, I didn't check the time but drank all six without any break or hesitation. I do not consider myself a lightweight, but the effect of that beer was immediate and profound! After what seemed to be five or seven minutes, I crushed my sixth can and looked at Johann with my head tilted to the side so that I could see only one of him!

He pointed and said, "Do you see those men?"

I saw seven, eight, or nine men in suits and asked, "How many are there?" He was typically all business with his answer.

"They are going to kill you if you don't kill them first."

I immediately started stumbling towards them as they pulled pistols out of their jackets. They were about ten yards away from me, and they didn't stand a chance! After I had a less than desirable time disarming them, I made them die of natural causes by shooting them in the head and or chest.

I went and stood in front of Johann. As I caught my breath by heavily gulping air, Johann pointed out to me and said, "That wasn't bad. You weren't hurt were you?"

"No, Johann."

"You're going to need a lot more training."

"I'm damn proud to serve you!"

§

The head of the Green Foot Family has absolute control over everything. To emphasize the total control that is exerted in the Green Foot Family, let me relate to you a horrifying experience that hasn't left me twenty-eight years later. Johann turned to the man standing next to him and said, "Take out your gun."

"I don't have a gun."

(Not everyone in the mob carries a gun. They all did in the beginning, but everyone gets promoted beyond that point, except for me. I never carried a single weapon ever.)

Johann turned to the man standing next to his unarmed servant and said, "Take out your gun." Upon completion of this order, Johann said, "Give it to him." (indicating the unarmed man)

Now the armed man was given the command, "Shoot yourself." –which he did. If people are willing to do this to themselves, what's to prevent them from injuring you!

Here is an example of one of the many experiences of my life in the Family. I had become a very light sleeper, and this made it easy for me to determine that someone was outside my bedroom door. I silently slipped into my large walk-in closet and became aware that some people entered my bedroom.

"Why are you here?"

"We're going to shoot you."

"No. I know that, but why?" I was given my death proclamation in one sentence.

"We heard you ate a pickle."

"That's the most expensive God damn pickle I ever heard of!"

I didn't bother telling them that I don't usually use profanity because I am fluent in two languages and I know enough words that I don't have to rely on swear words to express myself. They had come here to shoot me so I wasn't going to rely on their opinion of my lack of manners. I hope you, my reader, can understand me breaking from good form under slight duress.

"We're not getting paid. You aren't supposed to eat pickles, and we heard you ate a pickle today."

This how I knew there were five of them. I was able to quickly reenter the room before any of them said anything. I disarmed one, shot four (I always wonder how surprised someone is when I shoot them with their own gun!) and realized I might miss if I blindly shot at the back of the last one. I consider myself to be a man of integrity, which in turn, makes me quite trustworthy, but there is always a gray area where the mob is concerned. This is a lesson from the mob: If someone shoots at you once, that person will shoot at you again. Unless, of course, they're on your side and shooting in the same direction.

This was no small amount of excitement, and, although I can calm down very easily, the five or six men in white jumpsuits, who were the clean up crew, made it impossible for me to go right back to sleep. I'm glad I could watch the Sci-fi channel in the next room while they cleaned up.

Johann still used me as a negotiation tool, mob style, as he divided and gained criminal enterprises with other Green Foot Families. Sometimes, I was in one, two or three gunfights between 9:00-10:00pm to when my alarm went off at 5:00am. I was also in a few gunfights at any point during the day.

9

Johann had negotiations going on at all hours of the day. In addition to being an unpaid negotiation tool, I was tasked with eating and drinking what Johann wanted. A person may ask how I was able to financially sustain eating and drinking alcohol like the head of a Green Foot Family. Well, I still had my job of helping people arbitrate their differences for money. I worked for free ninety percent of the time, since I always believed in advertising as the best method for maintaining a loyal customer base. As a mercenary, I would charge between $1,000-$10,000 an hour the other ten percent of the time.

These payments were made in cash. Since I didn't have a source of employment that would justify having that much cash, it was all disposable income for me to spend only to support Johann's alcohol consumption. I couldn't keep any of the cash, so I bought rounds of beer for patrons at packed saloons and taverns. The bartenders, waiters, and waitresses loved it when I came in since they made more in tips from me in that one night then they did for the rest of the month.

A person would suppose that the Green Foot could fill the bill from my spending extravagances. Each man who participated in a gunfight would be paid $100,000. All other activities in the Green Foot made payments in percentages. If five men were told to go to a bank and were promised they'd be paid $100,000 each, they would only leave there with $500,000. But, if a man is a two-percenter, he's going to get two percent of $200,000 or $2,000,000. That's why they're encouraged to grab as much as they can of anything they can.

Unlike the military, there is no rank structure in the mob. If someone wanted to find out how the rank structure worked, they would have to look at the percentages. A fifteen-percenter is higher up than a ten-percenter who is higher up than a two-percenter. The lion's share goes to the head of the Family. The smuggling operations you read about in the newspaper, with the amount the government thinks the mob made, has ninety percent of that going to the head of the family. Everyone else gets a percentage of the last ten percent.

That's why mob wars are expensive and sought to be avoided. The Green Foot would go to whatever extent necessary to not pay their way. Their foundation is built on intimidation, fear and dishonesty.

Johann would appear in a crowded marketplace holding a briefcase. It was never my business as to how he did business. Remember that the head of the Family is given a "blank check" when it comes to their behavior. He would hold out the briefcase and say, "This is for you. It's $100,000."

I would take the briefcase and hold it while continuing to stare at him.

"Aren't you going to open it?"

"No. I trust you."

He always countered my naïve statement with, "Don't be doing that too much. Now, open it!" I would open a briefcase stacked with cash in the middle of a busy street or marketplace, and a uniformed police officer (never anyone that I recognized before or after) would walk up to me, take the briefcase, and walk away with it. Johann would start telling me how he wanted me to spend my money. I always asked if he was going to give me any money.

"I just gave you $100,000."

"The police officer has it."

"I gave it to you and you gave it to him."

I gave him the only answer I could. "I'm damn proud to serve you."

Here is another example of the arbitrary danger in the Green Foot. One day when I was alone in the house, there was a knock at the front door. I was curious as to why the doorbell wasn't used. When I opened the door, a man was standing at the front door. He was wearing a suit (the same color as his light brown hair and mustache) with white pinstripes. He was holding a pistol at a forty-five degree angle across his chest with his right hand and he was screwing on the silencer. I slammed the door and didn't lock it. This way I knew which direction he would be approaching from (this hit man had never been here before). I ran down the hallway about ten feet to the left of the front door. The hallway had a waist high wall on the left side. That wall separated the hallway from the dining room. The wall to the right was stone and also served as the backside of the fireplace in the next room. There's a door at the end of the stone wall that led me into the room that provided access to the beginning of the hallway that I had just run down.

The mustachioed man didn't register any surprise when he realized I was behind him. He spun around on the carpeted floor while extending the end of his pistol in his right hand toward my face. I used my left hand to push the back of his right hand while pressing the left side of the barrel with my right hand in the opposite direction. I was holding the pistol and didn't ask him what he was doing there. I have no idea what he thought when he went from predator to prey, as I shot him three times in rapid succession in the chest. He fell to the carpeted floor and blood poured out of the exit wounds in his back where the bullets exited his body.

He didn't lie there as long as a minute before three mustachioed men in white jumpsuits came to the front door. Two of them picked up the dead man while the third man had a large machine that had a metal cylinder about three feet long which looked like pogo stick handles on one end and a circle of brushes on the other end. In less than five minutes, there was no dead man and no sign of any blood.

These men all had mustaches for one reason only. As was told to me by Johann, ninety three percent of the time, an eyewitness will say that the suspect didn't have any facial hair.

The only real change happened when Johann didn't have any negotiations going on, and I had completed my initial service. In the Green Foot, everyone begins as a hit man or a negotiation tool. All men spend one to three years in these capacities. I was so good at what I did that I spent over two decades doing it. I didn't participate in all of the typical activities other than being in gunfights. I didn't drive slow enough on a consistent basis for anyone to trust me as a getaway driver and, because I walk with a limp, I couldn't take part in any bank robberies or anything else that would require not being easily recognized.

§

My traumatic brain injury prevented me from being of use in any smuggling operations or anything that required excruciating attention to detail. The getaway driver needs to have a valid driver's license (which I had), but needs to always drive slowly because if the police stop you, the police will win. I lasted through seven years as a negotiation tool before Johann kissed me on the check one day.   That was to signify that I had been promoted. He told me that the word had been put out that I would be able to assemble my own crew of two or three men who volunteered to serve him under my command. Sixty-eight hit men volunteered!

I got my first eight volunteers that night which is when the Green Foot does most of its work. I also wasn't told that anyone would be visiting me and that was also customary for the Green Foot and their dealings with me. I was in my bedroom with the lights on around one thirty in the morning, and there were seven women visiting me. I heard the door open and some people came into the room. I couldn't see who they were even though I was within six feet of the door. I heard a man ask where I was and someone must have pointed in my direction.

"He's on the bed? Two women at the same time and they're both on top? That's disgusting! We ought to shoot you just for that, but that's not why we're here."
I had my two female friends climb off me onto the other side of the bed. I got out of the bed to face the five men as the door closed behind them.

"Who just left?

"Three of them left when they saw you on the bed with those two women."

"Why are five of you here?"

"We want the chance to serve with Jimmy I. You're a legend."

I was never able to take a relationship with a woman to the next level because of what I did for a living. Not being able to share this was a death knell. How could I tell a woman that I was just in a gunfight and had to take out a few men because, as a mercenary, I had chosen Johann Goethe? I also had to talk to quite a few sketchy men at any time of the day or night and that would create fear and disassociation.

Being a mercenary for the Green Foot Family created unavoidable issues for a wife. The men in the family would have their wife and stay faithful to her. On the other hand, the wife could have an affair or several affairs over the course of their marriage and receive a hall pass. Divorce in the mob is never an option. To the

54

world, everything has to look perfect. This is the reason why I dated so many women. Marriage was never on the table.

I'm not a cold-hearted bastard. Yes, I was a mercenary for a living, but I had a few regrets when it came to the women I dated. There were one or two women that I would have happily spent the rest of my life with if my employment circumstances were different. Such is life.

Now I was in quite a dilemma. I had my own organized crime crew but, I had never done anything more than the gunfights where I was unarmed and on my own. Subsequently, I had to disarm and kill all of the men who were within five feet of me while they were shooting to kill. That's the way the Green Foot works. Everything is done on a sink or swim basis.

I continued to promote the cause of being a mercenary through helping people to arbitrate their differences for money. I was never paid to injure anybody, and I would protect my employer after they negotiated the terms of their peace. I was the bully to the bully, but I never carried a single weapon. I had studied or devised ways to disarm people with all forms of weapons because being a negotiation tool in the Green Foot meant that every form of weapon was used against me!

The list includes: pistols, shotguns, rifles (with or without bayonet), knives, machetes, swords, a garrote and brass knuckles. My success as a negotiation tool brought four offers from three other families to leave my service with Johann Goethe's family. My answer was always no, even though I was never able to spend any money that I made. Johann assured me that if I ever switched alliances, the Green Foot never forgets!

After I successfully prevented getting shot, I would disarm one of my assailants, shoot all four of them while continuing to avoid being shot, and then shoot the other head of the Green Foot Family. That's when I learned the cardinal rule of the Green Foot. Never injure the head of the Family. I had thought I was eliminating the threat to me, but my value to Johann's family is the only thing that prevented me from dying of natural causes at the hands of the other families. In the Green Foot, everything is considered death by natural causes. That includes a car bomb, a letter bomb, getting shot or stabbed or any other way that a person can die.

I had secondhand knowledge of all other Green Foot criminal enterprises from the head of the Family, Johann, but it was still secondhand information. I didn't know what to do since these killers did not appreciate any form of weakness and uncertainty, nor give any second chances. I know I mentioned quite a few times, "I'm damn proud to serve you!" This was my standard response when no other statement would suffice. I could never say, "Didn't you mean?" or "What did you say?" or "Are you sure?" They could never wonder about whose side I was on. My loyalty could never be in question.

I told some of these mobsters to meet me one night at the address of the restaurant that was out of business. I did not show up. Once this happened three times, they branded me an idiot and no longer wanted to serve me. But, they still feared me!

10

I have covered a copious amount of details in a very short space. I do believe

brevity is the soul of wit.' I will sum up the key points that I hope you take from my

experiences.

1. Mercenary means that you are working for payment only. That's it. The

    payment could be monetary compensation similar to when I was helping

    people arbitrate their differences for money, or the payment could be in

    the form of advice and/or guidance for living. I believe that living by arbitration is best. You provide whatever service you see yourself capable of providing for whatever form of payment you negotiate.

2. You are never paid to injure anyone.

3. The only thing that defines a person is what they're willing to do for what they believe in.

4. You can always renegotiate or reneg. Just make sure you're setting the terms.

5. If you're thinking about life in the world of criminal syndicates, or mob, the only advice you need to follow is DON'T DO IT. Life in the mob is not a recommended career choice for anyone. The only two reasons you would choose life in the criminal syndicate is to make a lot of money or to alter your personality

6. Be sure to take your studies seriously since you can never be sure when you will be touched by that fickle finger of fate.

If you get a job, show up and do your work. Do not spend all of your money between paychecks. You will make money. That's the basic principle. If you want to change yourself, there are plenty of twelve step programs that are free of charge and don't consider car bombs and letter bombs to be natural causes of death!

The End

ACKNOWLEDGEMENTS

A special thanks goes to Donna Valentino. Without you, this never could have gotten off the ground and come to fruition after I hand wrote the first draft.

Thanks to Johann Minx who told me, "Just start writing." You and Jacko Jaxson always lived up to your part in our friendship along with the 75-150 mercenaries I know.

Thanks to all my English teachers and German professors for all the great literature that you introduced me to, such as "The Divine Comedy" by Dante Alighieri.

Thanks to Camille Eisenkramer for your understanding when I told you that, "I can't come over since I am talking to Donna (Valentino).

Thanks to Dr. Kristen Innes for proofreading all the material for this book. "If you didn't want me to read it, you shouldn't have left it on the kitchen table."

Thanks to BIND (Brain Injury Network of Dallas) for introducing me to Donna Valentino and furthering my recovery after "My head eliminating half of the windshield of a car."

Made in the USA
Columbia, SC
09 May 2022

60102335R00035